GEORGE
AT THE
ZOO

GEORGE
AT THE
ZOO

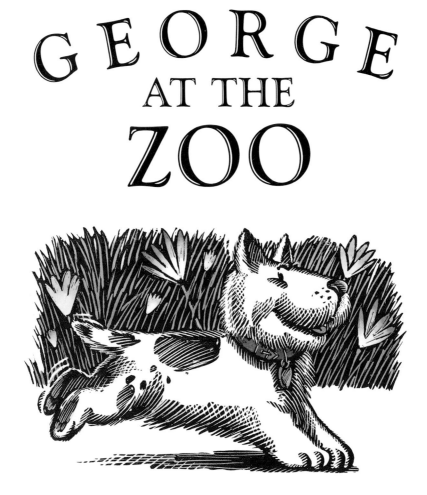

WRITTEN BY SALLY GEORGE
ILLUSTRATED BY ROB MANCINI

George was a small dog
who liked large bones
and going to picnics.
So when his family got out the picnic basket,
George got very excited.

"No, George!" said his family.
"We're going to the zoo.
Dogs can't go to the zoo."

But George liked
going in the car,
and smelling new smells,
and running in new places,
and, especially, eating the picnic.

So when his family wasn't looking,
George jumped inside the picnic basket.
The lid closed, and nobody saw him.

They picked up the picnic basket
and carried it out to the car.
It was very dark in the picnic basket.
And very crowded.

There was more room after George ate
the cold chicken,
and the ham,
and the rolls, and half the cake.

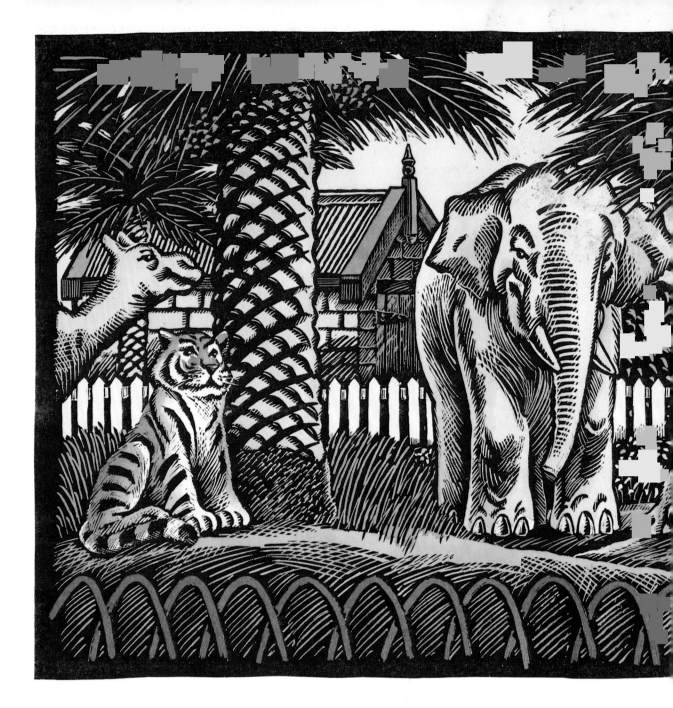

George's family went into the zoo.
"This is a very heavy picnic basket," they said.
But they didn't open it.
George pushed his nose through the lid.

He smelled lions and tigers,
and elephants and camels,
and bears and giraffes,
and emus and ostriches.

George liked the zoo.

His family walked and walked all over the zoo.
Finally, they sat down.
They opened the picnic basket.

"Oh, George!" they said.
"Bad dog, George!"

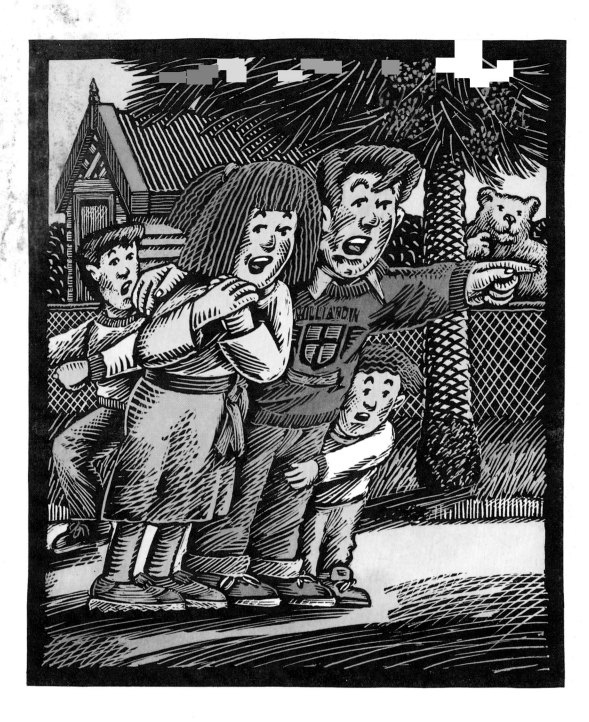

They were just about to shut the lid, when—
men began to shout,
women began to scream,
and children began to run.

George jumped out of the picnic basket.
There was the biggest cat he had ever seen.
And the cat had the biggest bone he had ever seen.

George forgot that he had just eaten
the cold chicken,
and the ham,
and the rolls, and half the cake.

George wanted that bone!

George's family sat in a tree and called him.
But George wanted that bone.

He growled and barked and snapped at the cat.
The cat came closer,
and roared back the biggest growl
that George had ever heard.

George growled and barked and snapped again.
The cat stopped,
and men came running
with trucks and ropes and nets,
and chased it into a big cage.

The men locked the cage with a big lock.
The men and the women and the children
stopped screaming.
Everyone looked at George.

George did not want to be chased
with trucks and ropes and nets
and be locked in a big cage.

He ran back to his picnic basket.

George's family got out of the tree.
He knew that they would say,
"Bad dog, George!"

But they didn't.
They seemed quite happy.
They said he was a good dog,
a wonderful dog,
the bravest,
best lion-chasing dog in the whole world.

Then they picked up the picnic basket
and carried it past the sign that said,
"No Dogs Allowed,"
and back to the car.

And when they got home,
George took the lion's bone
out of the picnic basket . . .

and buried it in the garden.